MY BEST FRIEND TONY SANTOS

Other *Best Friend* Books

My Best Friend, Duc Tran
    Meeting a Vietnamese-American Family

My Best Friend, Elena Pappas
    Meeting a Greek-American Family

My Best Friend, Martha Rodriguez
    Meeting a Mexican-American Family

MY BEST FRIEND TONY SANTOS

Meeting a Portuguese-American Family

PHYLLIS S. YINGLING

Pictures by Jan Palmer

Julian Messner ⓜ New York
A Division of Simon & Schuster, Inc.

Published by Julian Messner
A Division of Simon & Schuster, Inc.
Simon & Schuster Building
Rockefeller Center
1230 Avenue of the Americas
New York, NY 10020

JULIAN MESSNER and colophon are
trademarks of Simon & Schuster, Inc.

Designed by Meredith Dunham

Manufactured in the United States of America
10 9 8 7 6 5 4 3 2 1
Library of Congress Cataloging in Publication Data
Yingling, Phyllis S.
My best friend, Tony Santos.
Summary: A boy learns the family customs of his new
Portuguese-American friend.
1. Portuguese Americans—Social life and customs—
Juvenile literature. [1. Portuguese Americans—Social
life and customs] I. Title.
E184.P8Y56   1987   306'.08969073   87-7769
ISBN 0-671-63706-1

Contents

ACKNOWLEDGMENTS

Many people have graciously given their time and assistance in preparing this book. I am grateful to each of them.

In the Maryland suburbs of Washington, D.C.: Fr. Mario Lopez Martinez, the Rebelo Family, Abilio, Maria, and Filomena; Irene Ramos; and Maria Alho.

For information about soccer: Diane Barlow and Michael Artemis, as well as Drew Forrester of the Baltimore Blast.

In New Bedford, João Aguiar, Dineia Sylvia, Maria José Carvalho of Casa da Saudade; José and Maria Paiva and their children, Hugo and Lucianna; José Mota; Phyllis Stringer; and Robert Bruz.

A special thanks to Senhor Carlos Faria of the Portuguese Embassy staff and to Senhora Rita Pereira Bastos, wife of the ambassador from Portugal.

I appreciate Linda Beck's skills on the word processor and the enthusiastic support of my husband, Carroll, during the writing and research.

MY BEST FRIEND TONY SANTOS

1

Trick-or-Treat and *Pao-por-Deus*

What a soccer game that was today! The score was tied, three all, with only minutes to go. Kate had just tackled the ball and taken it away from the Tiger's center forward. She cleared the ball out to her sister, Taylor, who dribbled it down the field toward the Tiger's goal. Tony was sprinting down the field in the same direction. I ran to an open space in the middle of the field. Taylor sent a perfect pass to me. Now all I had to do was put the ball out in front of Tony, and he would have a shot on goal. But I mishit the ball. It took off straight for the Tiger's goalie. The goalie started out for the ball, but Tony ran like a fury and got there first. His hard, low shot went just under the goalkeeper's outstretched hand and into the net. The Cougars won! But I had almost lost the game for us with that bad pass.

We were sitting on the bench taking off our cleats and

shin guards when Chip Lewis, our coach, came toward us. He clapped Tony on the back. "Great goal, Santos!" he said, "Perfect shot."

Tony just grinned. "Thanks, Coach," he said.

Then Chip sat down beside me. "Ben, you've got to learn to get the ball under control before you try to pass it."

"Yes, sir," I said.

"It's okay, Ben," said Chip. "It's only a game. We'll work on your passing at practice. You've come a long way since last year."

Tony Santos is the best player the Cougars have. His family is from Portugal, and he's been playing soccer almost his entire life. He says his father started teaching him to kick a soccer ball as soon as he could walk. I just started playing last year.

We live in Maryland, just outside of Washington, D.C., and soccer is really big around here. All the neighborhoods have teams. I'd never played soccer before we moved here. I didn't even know that soccer is called football practically everywhere else in the world. Our American football is a totally different game. I really like to play soccer, but I don't think I'll ever be as good at it as Tony.

"How old are you, Tony?" Chip asked.

Tony said he'd be ten next month, in November.

"Then you should try out for the Rockets next summer," said Chip. "They could use a good forward like you."

"I'll be ten in December," I said kind of quietly.

The coach looked at me for a while. Then he said, "Well, Ben, maybe if you practice a lot between now and August you could make the Rockets' roster. But you know how it is. They choose only the very best players from the area."

The Riverview Rockets are a traveling team. That means they go all over the state playing other teams in the Maryland Youth Soccer Association. Anybody can play on a team like the Cougars, but you've got to be at least ten years old and really good to get a Rocket uniform.

As we walked home Tony said, "My Uncle Victor will help us get ready for the Rockets' tryouts. He's a great footballer. He played on a second-division team in Portugal. That's like semi-pro over here. With Uncle Victor's coaching we might both make the Rockets' team."

Tony's Uncle Victor lives with the Santos family. He came here from Portugal about five years ago to help Mr. Santos in his construction business. When we got to Tony's house, his Uncle Victor was raking leaves. Tony ran up to him and told him about how we won the game. Then he told him about the Rockets' tryouts and asked if he would coach us.

"*Sim.* Sure, sure!" Uncle Victor said. "I'll make you into a Rocket, Tonito. You, too, Ben. By August, the Rockets will be begging to have you on their team."

I smiled. They'll be begging for Tony, I thought, but not for me.

"You want to start practicing now?" asked Uncle Victor. "I can finish raking later. Let's go over to the empty lot next door."

"I'll phone my mom to see if it's okay for me to stay awhile," I said.

It was fine with Mom. She said she'd pick me up on the way home from the store.

Uncle Victor is a real pro. He showed me how to trap the ball between my feet before kicking it so I'd have more control. "You must develop a good foot," he said. "Learn to stop the ball, then kick it. When you kick, you should use the side of your foot."

After we'd practiced for about an hour, we went into Tony's house. Mrs. Santos made us some hot chocolate and brought out a plate of cookies that were like wafers. She called them *bolacha Maria* (boo LAH sha mah REE ah).

Just then the doorbell rang. It was my sister, Beth. "Come on, Ben," she said, "Mom's waiting in the car."

Mrs. Santos ran out the door and called, "Come in, Mrs. Elliott. The boys are having hot chocolate. Come have some, too."

So Mom and Beth came in, and Mrs. Santos got out more cookies and poured hot chocolate for everyone.

"How did the game go?" asked Beth. She's thirteen. She thinks sports are okay, but she'd rather sit home and read.

I told her how Tony's goal won the game for us, but I didn't mention that I'd messed up.

Tony asked, "Are you going to the Halloween party at the Rec Center next week, Ben?"

"Sure," I said. "You want to go together? I'm going as a pirate. What are you going to be?"

"I've got a blue jumpsuit. I'm going to wear it and Uncle Victor's motorcycle helmet and go as an astronaut," he said.

"That's a great idea! Are you going trick-or-treating with us before the party?" I asked.

"What's trick-or-treating?" asked Mrs. Santos.

I explained that back in the old days when my dad was young, kids used to play tricks on their neighbors—like putting the lawn furniture on the porch roof or soaping the car windows. Now kids go around the neighborhood knocking on doors and saying, "Trick or treat!" People give them treats so they won't play tricks on them. Nobody I know plays tricks like that anymore. And we also collect money for UNICEF, which helps kids all around the world.

Mrs. Santos smiled. "You know," she said, "in a way, this trick-or-treating reminds me of *pao-por-Deus*. That means "bread for God" in Portuguese. When I was a little girl in Portugal, we children went from house to house collecting "*pao-por-Deus*" in a bag. Most people gave us fruit and nuts. Afterward, we would take our bags to one person's house and divide everything we got among us."

"Did you do this on Halloween?" asked Beth.

"Oh, no," replied Mrs. Santos. "We collected the *pao-por-Deus* on All Saints Day, November first. That is a national holiday in Portugal. In the morning we would put on our best clothes and go to a special church service honoring all the saints. After that we went around the village collecting."

Then my mom said, "Thanks, Mrs. Santos, for the

cocoa and delicious cookies. I think we must be getting home now. I hope you'll drop by for a visit at our house some day. We're not far from here."

"That would be very nice," said Mrs. Santos. "It would be nice to get together more often."

As we left we saw Mr. Santos and Uncle Victor working in the yard. "*Adeus* (ah DAY osh), Ben," called Uncle Victor. "We will make you into a Rocket one day."

I waved as I got into the car. Maybe, I thought, but there are so many skills I've got to learn first. I dropped my cleats and shin guards on the floor of the car. I wanted to play for the Rockets more than anything else in the world!

2

Getting Ready for Pai Natal

Mrs. Santos invited our family to have dinner with them on Christmas Eve. She said it wouldn't be a big meal like Christmas dinner, but it was their traditional meal before they went to the Christmas Eve service at church.

On the morning of Christmas Eve, Beth and I went over to their house to see if we could help them get ready. We all decorated the Christmas tree and then set up the *Presepio* (pre ZE pu). That is what they call a Nativity scene in Portugal. First Tony laid a piece of plastic over a table near the tree. Then we covered it with moss, which Tony had brought in from the woods. We set the little *cabana* on the moss and placed the *Menino* Jesus and the figures of Maria and José inside. They are beautifully painted ceramic figurines about ten inches tall. Tony set the cow and donkey behind the manger. We put the shepherds and their sheep just outside the *cabana* looking in at the Menino. With some sand we made a road for the three *Magos* and their camels. It was a nice little scene. I felt like a friendly giant looking at real people.

Filomena, Tony's big sister, came into the room carrying a pair of shoes. "Don't forget your shoes, Tonito," she said.

Tony laughed. "I thought I was too big for that."

"I'm a student at the university," said Filomena, "but I wouldn't dare forget to leave my shoes for *Pai Natal* (pie NAH tahl)." She sounded very serious, but there was a smile on her face as she placed the shoes on the hearth beside the fireplace.

"Okay," said Tony, "if you're not too old, I guess I'm not either," and he dashed up the stairs.

"What are the shoes for?" asked Beth. "Are they like the stockings we hang up on Christmas Eve?"

"Exactly," said Filomena. "*Pai Natal* is what we call the gift bringer, like Santa Claus. Portuguese children set their shoes by the fireplace so he can leave presents in them."

Tony came downstairs carrying his best shoes in his hand.

"You think that new ten-speed you want will fit in those shoes?" asked his sister.

"About as well as the stereo cassette player you want will fit in yours," he replied.

Mrs. Santos walked into the room, wiping her hands on her apron. "Ten-speed bikes! Cassette players!" she exclaimed. "In my day, I was very happy to get a new dress for Christmas. My mother always made us something special to wear. Now you kids think Christmas is a time

for getting big, expensive gifts." She went over to the Nativity scene. "You did a nice job on the *Presepio*," she said to us. "This," she said, as she moved the baby a little closer to his mother, "is why we do all the celebrating. Remember that!" Then she gave Tony a little swat on his backside. "Ten-speeds! Stereos! Humph! Come help with the *filhos* (fee LYOSH)!"

The kitchen smelled wonderful. Mrs. Santos had spent the morning baking the *bolo rei* (bo loo RAY). It was a fruitcake made with yeast, a special treat for Christmas dinner.

"Last year at my sister's house I got the *fava* (FAH vah)," said Mrs. Santos.

"That's the one broad bean that is mixed into the dough before the *bolo rei* is baked," Filomena explained. "The person who gets that bean has to provide the cake for next year's Christmas dinner."

"Let's get to work on the *filhos*," said Tony. "This is my favorite thing about Christmas Eve."

Mrs. Santos had made a batter of flour, eggs, yeast, and a dash of brandy earlier in the morning. Now the yeast had made it soft and puffy. We each took turns dropping some of the batter into hot oil. When the *filhos* were golden brown, we removed them from the oil and let them drain on paper towels. Then we rolled them in sugar and spice. Oh, wow! Were they good! It was hard not to eat them all up as we made them.

The meal that evening was great! We had broccoli, potatoes, and codfish that had all been boiled together. Codfish, or *bacalhau* (ba cah LYOW), as they call it, is one of the favorite foods of Portuguese people. Mrs. Santos says she's glad there are so many ways to fix it, because her family likes to have *bacalhau* at least once a week. She had mixed together a sauce of olive oil, vinegar, and pepper, which we sprinkled over the fish and vegetables. There was also some of Mrs. Santos' famous homemade *pao*. For dessert we had a lemony rice pudding called *arroz doce* (ah ROSH DO suh) and some of those yummy *filhos*. I couldn't imagine how Christmas dinner could top that meal.

That evening when we left, Tony called, "*Feliz Natal,* everybody!" "And Merry Christmas to you," I shouted back.

The next morning I saw Tony riding up and down the street on a shiny new bike. I tried to imagine how it could have fit into his shoes.

3

Uncle Victor Becomes an American Citizen

Last night my dad drove over to Baltimore to a Blast game. The Baltimore Blast is a professional indoor soccer team. They were playing a team that has a Portuguese player who is a friend of Uncle Victor. The Blast won! Afterward, we went down to the locker room and met Uncle Victor's friend and got autographs from all of the players.

On the way home, Uncle Victor said he had been in Baltimore just the week before. He had applied to become a naturalized citizen at the United States Office of Immigration there. He's lived in the United States more than five years now, so last fall he got the application forms for citizenship. He's been studying English at night at the high school. At the library he got books that helped him learn about American history and government.

"Did you have to take a test?" I asked.

"Yes," answered Uncle Victor, "but it wasn't as hard as I thought it would be. They only asked three questions. What is the highest court in the land was one of them."

"The Supreme Court," answered Tony quickly.

"How long can a president stay in office?" continued Uncle Victor, "And who is the vice president?"

"That's not so bad," said Dad. "I always thought it was a long, written test."

"Believe me," said Tony's dad, "when you are new to a country and you don't know the language so well, it is very hard to answer even three or four questions. I remember how scared I was when I had my interview. You must also show that you can write and speak in English."

"Are you a citizen now?" Beth asked Uncle Victor.

"No, I must wait for my papers to be processed. They said it would take about eight months. Maybe by August I will be sworn in as a United States citizen."

"Boy, I bet you can hardly wait," I said.

"It is not an easy thing to decide," said Uncle Victor. "When I swear allegiance to the United States of America, I will have to give up my Portuguese citizenship. That is a hard thing to do. Portugal is where I was born. It is my beloved homeland."

"I thought you could have dual citizenship," said Beth.

"No, the United States does not recognize dual citizenship. When I become a U.S. citizen, I will no longer be a citizen of Portugal."

Everyone was quiet for a while. I thought about how hard it would be to give up my American citizenship. It would be a tough decision.

"So, what is everybody going to do for *Carnaval* (cahr nah VAHL)?" asked Mr. Santos, changing the subject.

"What is *Carnaval*?" I asked. "Is that when you have a Ferris wheel, merry-go-round, and other rides? Like the fireman's carnival?"

"No," laughed Tony, as he gave me a poke in the arm. "It's car*na*val. It's like a celebration before Lent begins. You know, getting ready for Easter."

"I saw a program on television about the Carnaval in Rio," said Beth. "It was really wild!"

"That's right," said Filomena. "Everybody gets a little bit crazy. Last year I was in Lisboa for *Carnaval,* and it was marvelous. There were parades with everyone dressed up in outrageous costumes and fantastic floats and dozens of bands. People were dancing in the streets and having a wonderful time. I loved it!"

"Here in Riverview," said Tony, "we have a really big party at the fire hall. We all get dressed up in the weirdest costumes we can dream up. Sometimes, when the weather is not too cold, we dance in the street too. It's lots of fun.

"Last year I dressed up like a scarecrow," Tony went on. "I took an old sheet and put it over my head. *Mai* cut slits for my eyes and mouth. Filomena put lipstick all around the mouth slit. Then I put on one of *Pai*'s old shirts and a pair of his pants."

"We stuffed a pillow inside his shirt," said Filomena, "to make him look fat. Then we pulled one of *Pai*'s old hats down on his head and put *Mai*'s garden gloves on his hands." She laughed. "He looked just like the scarecrow from *The Wizard of Oz.*"

14

15

"Do grown-ups go to the party, too?" I asked.

"Oh, sure," answered Mr. Santos. "Everybody goes. Old people. Kids. Everyone." Looking at his brother, he added, "Victor, here, likes to go and *samba* with all the pretty ladies. Right, Victor?"

Uncle Victor just smiled and nodded his head.

"Is there a real band?" I asked.

"Definitely," said Filomena. "They play all kinds of music. Portuguese songs and Brazilian *sambas,* as well as American pop. It's great fun! Everybody eats and drinks and dances. The little kids all chase each other around. You'll love it!"

"You won't recognize the fire hall," said Tony. "It will be all decorated with balloons and streamers of all colors. It always looks great."

"Is it okay if I go, Dad?" I asked.

"Sounds good to me," he said.

"You come, too," Mr. Santos said to Dad. "Bring the whole family."

Now I can hardly wait until next Saturday night and the *Carnaval* dance. It's fun being friends with the Santos family.

4

A Visit to the Portuguese Embassy

I am really tired. My feet and legs feel like I've walked a hundred miles. This was the day of our class field trip to Washington, D.C. Boy, did we have fun! We've been studying about our government. In the morning we went to visit the United States Capitol. It is such a big building! A couple of times I almost got lost.

After lunch, the bus took us to the Portuguese Embassy. Since we have four kids in our class who are from Portuguese-American families, our teacher Ms. DeHaven thought it would be a good idea for all of us to learn something about the Portuguese government, too. She had already taught us about Prince Henry the Navigator and the Portuguese explorers, Bartolomeu Dias (bar too loo MAYOO DEE ush) and Vasco de Gama (VASH KOO dah GAH mah), in social studies. They were the first Europeans to find a way to sail around Africa to get to India and

China. That was before Christopher Columbus discovered America. I was surprised to learn that Columbus had gone to Portugal to study navigation before he set sail across the Atlantic Ocean.

I thought the embassy would be just another office building. Ms. DeHaven had explained that most governments of the world have people who represent them in our capital city. The person in charge is called the ambassador. The United States has embassies all over the world, too. That's how different countries work together.

Although there are offices in an attached building, the Portuguese Embassy is really a big mansion where the ambassador and his family live. The Portuguese flag fluttered over the heavy, wooden front doors as we gathered on the steps. The ambassador's wife welcomed us. *"Boa tarde,"* she said. "Good afternoon." She was a beautiful lady. She shook hands with our teacher and asked us all to come in.

We all went trooping into a huge hall and began looking around. Ms. DeHaven told the *Senhora* about the Portuguese-American kids in our class. The ambassador's wife spoke to each of them in Portuguese. I was impressed when they answered her in Portuguese.

A man from the embassy staff joined us. He led us into a large living room with beautiful furniture. On one of the tables there was a very old, odd-shaped box. In it was a strange instrument. The *Senhora* explained that it was a sextant like the ones those early explorers used to navigate their ships all around the world. By focusing the sextant on the sun or a star, the sailors could find out the position

of their ship. She also showed us a small marble statue of Prince Henry looking out to sea.

We went through a door into another huge room. It was even grander than the first. It looked like a room in a palace. It had beautiful antique furniture in it, and there was a gigantic tapestry on the wall. I could just imagine a fancy party in there with diplomats and government officials talking about politics.

The room I liked best was the dining room. Everything in it was made in Portugal. It had the biggest table I ever saw. I bet you could seat thirty people around it. It was made of a special wood from Brazil. There were beautiful blue ceramic tiles all around the lower part of the walls. Portugal is famous for the ceramics made there.

When we returned to the entrance hall, the man from the embassy staff asked if we had any questions. I asked if Portugal's government is like ours. He explained that Portugal is a republic with an elected president and parliament. The parliament is made up of representatives like our Congress. They also have a prime minister who is appointed by parliament. The supreme court makes up the third branch of government, just like ours.

Charles said he has a pen-friend in Brazil. He wondered why the people of Brazil speak Portuguese. The *Senhor* told us that Brazil was discovered by the Portuguese explorer, Pedro Cabral (PEH droo kah BRAHL), in 1500. Many Portuguese people settled there. The Portuguese colonists brought their language to the New World just as the British settlers brought English to the thirteen original colonies of the United States. Now, like the United States,

Brazil is an independent nation, but the people still speak the language of those early settlers.

Before we left, the ambassador's wife shook hands with each of us. Ms. DeHaven thanked her for allowing our class to visit the embassy. As we went out the door, Tony said, "*Obrigado* (oh bree GAH doo), *Senhora.*"

She gave him a little hug and said to all of us, "Thank *you* for coming. *Adeus.*"

"*Adeus, Senhora,*" we called back to her.

That was one of the best field trips we've ever had. I'd like to go there again.

When we got home from the trip, Tony and I went over to the vacant lot to practice soccer. We had marked off a goal with some rocks. We passed the ball to each other, then shot it between the rocks. At least we tried to shoot it between the rocks. When Uncle Victor got home from work, he came over and watched us. I kept missing the goal or shooting too high.

"Keep your eyes on the ball," called Uncle Victor. "Shoot hard. Keep it low."

I tried and tried. Just about the time I thought I was doing better, I'd lose control and the ball went everywhere except in the goal.

Uncle Victor said, "Ben, you must practice juggling. Everyday when you come home from school, work on keeping the ball in the air. That is how you learn to control the ball. Then he showed us how he juggles. First he kicked the soccer ball up in the air with his knee, then his toe, then his shoulder, the back of his leg, his head, his other knee, his toe again. On and on. I think he could have kept that ball in the air forever. But just then Tony's mother called them to come home and eat supper.

Maybe, one day, if I practice and practice hard enough. I'll begin to feel confident with the ball. I'm determined to make the Rockets' team!

I picked up the ball and kicked it with my knee. Then I kicked it with my toe. I think I'm beginning to learn.

5

New Bedford and the Fishing Fleet

I couldn't believe it when Tony's parents asked my folks if I could go to New Bedford, Massachusetts, with them to visit relatives. I was even more amazed when my mom and dad said it was okay with them.

We left on a steaming hot day in August. The trip to Massachusetts was exciting. It was my first trip in a camper.

When we pulled into Tony's cousin's driveway, the whole family came out to greet us. Everybody hugged everybody else, the way all families do. When Tony introduced me, I got hugged, too. They welcomed me in English, but before long the grown-ups were chatting away in Portuguese. Mrs. Santos and her sister, Celia, were so happy to see each other. Tony's cousin, José (Joo SEH), is about the same age as we are, but his little sister, Maria, is only five years old. Tony and José spoke mostly in English, but once in a while they'd slip into Portuguese. I felt as if I were in a foreign country. I know a few Portuguese words, but not enough to use in conversation.

Tia Celia said she was sorry that José's dad wasn't there to greet us. He was out on the boat fishing and would not be back for several days. He is a commercial fisherman. That means it's his job. He catches fish to sell to restaurants and stores. He doesn't just go out fishing for fun.

"How long do they stay out?" I asked.

"Oh, eight to ten days," said José. "Then they stay home for three or four days and get the boat ready to go out again."

"When they stay out so long, where do they sleep? How do they have enough food to eat?" I wanted to know.

José laughed. "They eat and sleep on the boat," he said. "It's a very big boat. You'll see it when they come home."

"How many men work with Manuel (mah noo EL)?" asked Mr. Santos.

"There are six of them," answered Tia Celia. "They are a good crew. They work well together."

That evening the Santos family took us all out to eat dinner. We went to one of the many Portuguese restaurants in town. A dark-haired man sang *fado** songs in one corner of the room. As he sang, he accompanied himself on a Portuguese guitar. It was beautiful music. Tia Celia said *fado* is like Portuguese "soul music."

The food was good. Tony and I ate kale soup, *fava* beans cooked in a spicy sauce, and *carne guisada*. Mr. Santos ordered *cabrito*, and Tia Celia had *coelho*. They are

24

special foods of the Portuguese who come from the island of Madeira. I was surprised when Maria asked for a hamburger, and José got steak and french fries. I guess they are becoming typical American kids.

The next day we untied our bikes from the back of the camper, and the three of us rode over to *Casa da Saudade* (KA za dah so THA duh). José says that means "house of memories." It reminds the Portuguese Americans of their hometowns back in Portugal. More than half of the people in the city are from Portugal or the islands belonging to Portugal. The *Casa da Saudade* is really a library where you can get books in either English or Portuguese. We checked out some Portuguese magazines for José's mother. José introduced us to the director of the library and his assistants. They explained how the *Casa* offers programs to help the Portuguese immigrants learn English and study for the test they take when they become naturalized United States citizens.

After lunch we all went to visit the Whaling Museum. A hundred years ago, New Bedford was the center of the whaling industry. Before there was electricity, people used whale oil to light their lamps. Catching whales and melting down their blubber into oil was very important work. We saw a film about whaling at the museum. Many of the first Portuguese came to America on whaling ships. The captains of the ships stopped at the Azores, Madeira, or the Cape Verde Islands for supplies. Many of the young men from those islands joined the crews of the whaling ships. Later, after they had settled in America, they sent for their families.

That's the way it was with José's family. His father was a fisherman in a small village on the coast of Portugal. Five years ago a relative told him about New Bedford. He and Tia Celia came here to see if he could find work and a place to live. José stayed back in the village with his grandparents. When his dad got work on a fishing boat and they found a house to live in, his parents sent for José. I asked him if he liked the trip over on the plane. He shook his head no. He was only five years old at the time. I guess such a long trip alone to a new country would be pretty scary.

The next day Tio Manuel came home. Everyone was so glad to see him, especially little Maria. She ran to him as soon as he walked in the door calling, *"Pai! Pai!"* Her father tossed her up in the air and then held her in his arms while he greeted all of us.

Tio Manuel told us about the trip. They had a big catch of yellowtails, flounder, and codfish. Now they will stay home for a few days to mend their nets and scrub down the boat. The coming weekend was the Blessing of the Fleet, so they wanted to get the *Alice Maria* (ah LEE seh mah REE ah) all shipshape by Sunday.

On Saturday we all went down to help work on the boat. There would be a prize for the best decorated boat. I was surprised at how big the fishing boats were. We climbed aboard the *Alice Maria,* and José took us on a tour. Below deck there was a galley the size of my mom's kitchen. It had plenty of room for six men to eat. Beyond the galley were three cabins. In each little room there were double-decker beds and storage space for the crew's gear.

Up on the bridge, it looked like the cockpit of an airplane. There were all kinds of dials and radar screens. That's where the pilot stands. Tio Manuel let me turn the huge wheel a little. I pretended I was the captain of a ship steering out into the Atlantic Ocean.

Sunday dawned bright and hot. It was a perfect day to be out on the water. All the fishing boats were freshly painted or scrubbed spanking clean. Brightly colored pennants whipped from lines stretched high above their decks. Portuguese and American flags flew from their sterns. At two o'clock the boats chugged out into the river forming a broad arc. Then, one after another, they turned, heading back toward the wharf where a Coast Guard ice breaker was moored. On board the Coast Guard ship, a band played patriotic marches. The judges made notes on the beauty and creativity of each boat's trimmings. Three priests, two Catholic and one Greek Orthodox, held *aspergilles* of holy water. As each boat cruised by the bow of the ice breaker, the priests sprinkled its deck and offered a word of blessing.

All of the boats were filled with the fishermen and their families and friends. Everyone was laughing and singing and waving to friends on shore. As we drifted closer to the Coast Guard ship, I noticed Tia Celia gathered José and Maria to her side. The three of them bowed their heads for a moment as the priest prayed for the safety and success of the boat and its crew. When we had passed beyond the priests, Tio Manuel at the wheel gave three long blasts on the horn.

The rest of the afternoon was so much fun! All of the

men in the crew had their families with them. I got to meet lots of kids. José's best friend, Hugo, is a great soccer player. He and José and Tony and I had joined in some pick-up games on the school soccer field the last few days. I had been feeling pretty good about my juggling and passing, but I couldn't compare to those guys. It was only two more weeks until the Rockets' tryouts. I just couldn't tell if I would be picked for the team.

Tio Manuel headed down the river and out into Buzzard's Bay toward the islands. Tia Celia and the other women had fixed tons of food. We all ate until we were too stuffed to move. Sea gulls followed the boats, noisily gathering scraps that were tossed their way. Later in the afternoon, as we sailed past Martha's Vineyard, José and I gathered up empty soda cans. After tying strings around them we dropped them over the side of the boat and brought them up full of water. Then we crept up behind Hugo and Tony and poured it over their heads. Naturally, they had to get us back.

We chased each other all over the boat until one of the girls put ice down José's shirt. That started a whole new game. We grabbed chunks of ice from the ice chest and ran after the girls. They scattered in every direction, giggling and screaming. Finally, Tio Manuel told us to cut it out and swab the decks where we'd made a mess. Tia Celia set out the food that was left, and everyone ate and drank some more. That's an afternoon I'll never forget! As we motored back into the harbor at sunset I wished we could stay on board the *Alice Maria* forever.

6

Celebration!

Did you ever notice that when you're in school the months seem to crawl by slowly? On the other hand, July and August whiz by like engines racing to a fire. I can't believe that September is almost here. It's been a great summer! And this last week has topped it off perfectly.

On Thursday we went to Baltimore with the Santos family to attend the ceremony that made Uncle Victor a United States citizen.

It was very impressive when he stood before the judge with the other people from different countries. All of them raised their right hands and pledged their allegiance to the United States of America. It was a very special moment for each of us.

To celebrate Uncle Victor's citizenship, Tony's family planned a picnic in their back yard. Our family was invited along with some other friends and neighbors. We had codfish cakes and *carne de espeto,* which Mr. Santos cooked over the grill. Tony wanted hot dogs and hamburgers, so we had a real Portuguese-American picnic, right down to *pasteis de nata* and watermelon for dessert.

After eating, Uncle Victor got out his guitar and sang some Portuguese songs that brought tears to Mrs. Santos' eyes. Then he taught us all a couple of funny folk songs. Next thing you know we were singing "I've Been Working on the Railroad" and "She'll be Coming 'Round the Mountain." We had just started "Home on the Range" when our coach, Chip Lewis, came around the corner of the house.

"Hi, everybody," he said. "I hope I'm not intruding."

"No, no," said Mrs. Santos. "Come have some watermelon."

"Thanks, Mrs. Santos," he said, "but I really just stopped by to congratulate the new citizen." He shook Uncle Victor's hand. "I'm happy you decided to make it official."

Then he turned to Tony and said, "I also want to offer congratulations to the Rockets' newest center forward. You were outstanding at the tryouts last week, Tony!"

Tony grinned at his dad. "I made it!"

His dad gave him a friendly poke in the arm. "I knew you would, Tonito," he said. "There was never any doubt in my mind."

"That's great, Tony," I said. "You'll make a terrific center."

I had a terrible feeling in the pit of my stomach, but I really was glad Tony had made the team. After all, he is my best friend.

Chip grabbed my hand. "And congratulations to the Rockets' newest fullback. You made the roster, too, Ben!"

It's dumb to feel like crying when you're so happy, but I almost did. Tony grabbed me, and we jumped around the way we do when our team scores a goal.

My dad said, "Well, it looks as if the Rockets will have a winning team this year!" and clasped Tony and me around the shoulders. Beth grinned, and Mom laughed as she said, "I guess that means you'll be late for dinner every Saturday this fall!"

We all just stood there for a moment grinning at each other. It felt like the Fourth of July and Christmas all in one. There should have been fireworks!

"Say, how about a little pick-up game?" called Uncle Victor.

Before long we were all in the vacant lot next door playing the wildest soccer match you ever saw!

GLOSSARY

adeus (ah DAY osh)—goodbye.

aspergilles (AS per jil es)—liturgical instruments used for sprinkling holy water.

Açores (uh SORSH)—a group of islands in the Atlantic Ocean west of Portugal and belonging to Portugal.

boa tarde (BOH ah TAR duh)—good afternoon.

cabana kah BAN nah)—a small house.

cabrito (kah BREE toh)—tender young goat cooked in tomatoes, herbs, and spices.

Cape Verde Islands—a group of islands in the Atlantic Ocean off the west coast of Africa that were possessions of Portugal.

carne guisada (KAR nay GWEE sat da)—stewed beef.

carne de espeto (kar nay desh PEH teh)—barbecued cubes of beef.

coelho (ku AY loo)—stewed rabbit.

Deus (DAY ohsh)—God.

fado (FAH'doh)—a type of Portuguese folk music.

Feliz Natal (feh LEESH nah TAHL)—Happy Christmas.

Lisboa (LEESH boah)—Lisbon, the capital city of Portugal.

Madeira (mah DAY rah)—a group of five islands off the northwest coast of Africa that belong to Portugal.

Magos (MAH goosh)—Magi, the wise men who visited Bethlehem at the birth of Jesus.

mai (MAH ee)—mother.

menino (meh NEE noo)—child.

obrigado (oh bree GAH doo)—thank you.

pai (pie)—father.

Pai Natal (pie nah TAHL)—Father Christmas.

pao (pown)—bread.

pasteis de nata (pahs STEHS duh NAH tah)—Portuguese cookies.

samba (SAHM ba)—a Brazilian dance.

senhor (sen YOR)—mister.

senhora (sen YOR ah)—madame or Mrs.

sim (seeng)—yes.

tia (TEE ah)—aunt.

tio (TEE oh)—uncle.

About the Author

Phyllis Stuckey Yingling is a teacher in Baltimore, Maryland. She is the author of *My Best Friend Elena Pappas* and has written articles and stories for educational and religious publications as well as stories for children's magazines such as *Highlights for Children, Ranger Rick,* and *Humpty Dumpty.* For an article about Jane Addams, she won the *Highlights for Children* Biography of the Year Award in 1984. She lives in Baltimore with her husband, Carroll. Their children, Beth and Lewis (Chip), are married and establishing families of their own.